Piggy
Let's Be Friends!

TREVOR LAI

BLOOMSBURY
NEW YORK LONDON OXFORD NEW DELHI SYDNEY

Copyright © 2018 by Trevor Lai
All rights reserved. No part of this book may be reproduced or transmitted in any form or by any means,
electronic or mechanical, including photocopying, recording, or by any information storage and
retrieval system, without permission in writing from the publisher.

Published in the United States of America in February 2018
by Bloomsbury Children's Books
www.bloomsbury.com

Bloomsbury is a registered trademark of Bloomsbury Publishing Plc

For information about permission to reproduce selections from this book, write to
Permissions, Bloomsbury Children's Books, 1385 Broadway, New York, New York 10018
Bloomsbury books may be purchased for business or promotional use. For information on bulk purchases
please contact Macmillan Corporate and Premium Sales Department at specialmarkets@macmillan.com

Library of Congress Cataloging-in-Publication Data
Names: Lai, Trevor, author, illustrator.
Title: Piggy : let's be friends! / by Trevor Lai.
Other titles: Let's be friends!
Description: New York : Bloomsbury, 2018.
Summary: Piggy and Kate invite Miles, a mole who is afraid to come out of the ground, to a tea party with all of their friends.
Identifiers: LCCN 2017019948 (print) | LCCN 2017036727 (e-book)
ISBN 978-1-68119-068-6 (hardcover)
ISBN 978-1-68119-069-3 (e-book) • ISBN 978-1-68119-070-9 (e-PDF)
Subjects: | CYAC: Pigs—Fiction. | Moles (Animals)—Fiction. | Bashfulness—Fiction. | Friendship—Fiction. | Forest animals—Fiction.
Classification: LCC PZ7.1.L23 Pik 2018 (print) | LCC PZ7.1.L23 (e-book) | DDC [E]—dc23
LC record available at https://lccn.loc.gov/2017019948

Art created in pencil and watercolor and then finished digitally
Typeset in Jolly Good Proper
Book design by John Candell
Printed in China by Leo Paper Products, Heshan, Guangdong
2 4 6 8 10 9 7 5 3 1

All papers used by Bloomsbury Publishing, Inc, are natural, recyclable products
made from wood grown in well-managed forests. The manufacturing processes
conform to the environmental regulations of the country of origin.

Piggy lived in the heart of the forest.

He was once a lonely pig, surrounded only by his books.

Then, he met his best friend, Kate. The more they shared, the more friends they made.

Soon, Piggy was friends with everyone in the forest.
Well, *almost* everyone . . .

Miles was a mole who was always alone.

He did not know anyone in the forest, because he lived *under* it.

Miles wanted to see the world above, but it made him too
nervous. And when Miles felt nervous, he sneezed—*AACHOOO!*

One day, Miles's nose was tickled
by a scent.
He followed the lovely smell and
peeked out of the hole. Someone
was there!

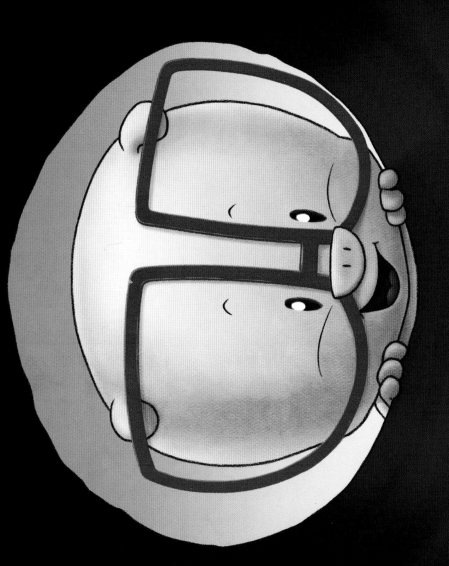

Piggy heard a loud *AACHOOO!*

"Hello, is anyone down there?" Piggy shouted.

Miles was too nervous to reply. *AACHOOO!*

"My name is Piggy. Do you have a name?" Piggy asked.

"M-m-m-maybe my name . . . is Miles. *AACHOOO!*

Good-bye!"

Piggy wondered
who Miles was.

Did he like to read books?

*What did he do
underground?*

Would he come back?

Meanwhile, Miles
wondered about Piggy, too.

*Was he
friendly?*

*What did
Piggy do all day
in the sun?*

Would they see each other again?

Later that day, Piggy and Kate were busy
preparing for a tea party.
The smell of Kate's blueberry muffins led Miles
above ground again.

Piggy saw him and called out, "Hi, Miles!"

"Come to our tea party tomorrow!" said Piggy. "You can meet our friends."

Miles felt a sneeze tickling his nose—"*Ah…Ah…*"

Then, Kate handed him a muffin. The delicious scent calmed him down.

"You can have more tomorrow!" Kate smiled.

"M-m-m-maybe . . . good-bye!" Miles said before he jumped back into his hole.

Miles wondered if it might be safer to stay home.

But there are never any tea parties underground, he thought.

Finally, Miles knew what would make his new friends happy.
He couldn't wait to see them again!

On the day of the party, the smell of roses and blueberries filled the air.

Miles peeked at all of Piggy's friends.
The little mole took a deep breath and
popped out of his hole.

Suddenly, he felt a bit shy.
And then a bit nervous.
And then—**AACHOOO!**

The cake landed on the little mole's head.
Before Piggy could say anything, the Bunny Brothers started laughing.

"Who is that?"
"Why is he so dirty?"

Miles jumped back into his hole.

"Wait, don't leave!" Piggy called out.

"We're sorry," said Big Brother Bunny. "We didn't mean to scare him away."

"All he wanted was to have friends like us," said Piggy.

"There must be something we can do!" exclaimed Kate.

Piggy wondered, *What would make Miles happy?*

Then, Piggy had a plan!

Miles was alone again.
He wished he had never
gone above ground.

Just when he felt lonelier
than ever before, Miles's nose
was tickled by a scent.

Suddenly, Piggy and all his
friends appeared.
"Surprise!" they cheered.

Piggy and his friends
made the underground home
brighter and happier.

Together with Miles, they had their
first underground tea party ever.

Piggy lived in the heart of the forest, and he was friends with everyone . . .

. . . including Miles. And the little mole never felt alone again.